Dear Parent:

Congratulations! Your child is taking the first steps on an exciting journey. The destination? Independent reading!

STEP INTO READING® will help your child get there. The program offers five steps to reading success. Each step includes fun stories and colorful art. There are also Step into Reading Sticker Books, Step into Reading Math Readers, Step into Reading Phonics Readers, Step into Reading Write-In Readers, and Step into Reading Phonics Boxed Sets—a complete literacy program with something for every child.

Learning to Read, Step by Step!

Ready to Read   Preschool–Kindergarten
• big type and easy words • rhyme and rhythm • picture clues
For children who know the alphabet and are eager to begin reading.

Reading with Help   Preschool–Grade 1
• basic vocabulary • short sentences • simple stories
For children who recognize familiar words and sound out new words with help.

Reading on Your Own   Grades 1–3
• engaging characters • easy-to-follow plots • popular topics
For children who are ready to read on their own.

Reading Paragraphs   Grades 2–3
• challenging vocabulary • short paragraphs • exciting stories
For newly independent readers who read simple sentences with confidence.

Ready for Chapters   Grades 2–4
• chapters • longer paragraphs • full-color art
For children who want to take the plunge into chapter books but still like colorful pictures.

STEP INTO READING® is designed to give every child a successful reading experience. The grade levels are only guides. Children can progress through the steps at their own speed, developing confidence in their reading, no matter what their grade.

Remember, a lifetime love of reading starts with a single step!

Step into Reading, Random House, and the Random House colophon are registered trademarks of
Random House LLC.

Visit us on the Web!
StepIntoReading.com
randomhouse.com/kids

Educators and librarians, for a variety of teaching tools, visit us at RHTeachersLibrarians.com

ISBN 978-0-385-37434-7 (trade) – ISBN 978-0-385-37435-4 (lib. bdg.)

Printed in the United States of America   10 9 8 7 6 5 4 3 2

nickelodeon
TEENAGE MUTANT NINJA
TURTLES

DOUBLE-
TEAM!

Adapted by Christy Webster
Illustrated by Patrick Spaziante

Based on the teleplay "Mousers Attack!" by Kenny Byerly

Random House 🏠 New York

Late one night, the Teenage Mutant Ninja Turtles were in their lair. Their teacher, Splinter, led them in a practice drill.

"Are you fighting in slow motion?" Raphael teased Leonardo.

"I could go faster if I ignored my form, like you," Leo replied.

"Ignore *this* form!" With that, Raph attacked Leo, and they continued sparring.

Splinter grabbed the two Turtles, stopping their fight. "You must learn to work together," he said. "Spar two-on-two against Donatello and Michelangelo."

"Is that fair?" asked Raphael. "We're way better."

Mikey scoffed. "At fighting, maybe."

"That's what I meant," Raph said.

Splinter signaled them to begin. Mikey and Donnie were on the floor in seconds.

"You were right, Sensei," said Raphael. "Working together is fun."

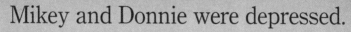

Mikey and Donnie were depressed.

"Look, guys," Leo said. "Raph and I are better fighters, but you are still important to this team."

"You two think of us as some kind of B team," Mikey said.

April came into the lair, looking upset.
"What's wrong?" asked Donnie.
"Some guys from the Purple Dragons mugged me," April said. The Purple Dragons were a dangerous street gang. "They took my phone."
The Turtles wanted to get April's phone back, but Splinter urged them to stay put.

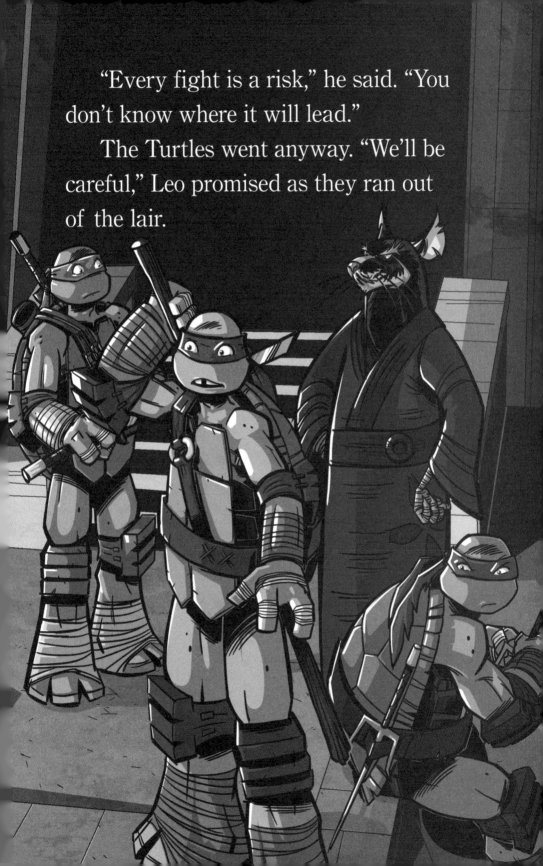

"Every fight is a risk," he said. "You don't know where it will lead."

The Turtles went anyway. "We'll be careful," Leo promised as they ran out of the lair.

The Turtles found Fong, Sid, and Tsoi, members of the Purple Dragons, in their hideout.

THWACK! Raphael kicked Sid in the chest. Fong and Tsoi tried to fight back, but Leo and Raph shut down their every move. Mikey and Donnie couldn't even get one hit in.

"We want our friend's phone back," Leo said.

The defeated Dragons showed the Turtles their back room. It was full of stolen phones and other gadgets.

Donnie pointed to a red phone with a charm on it. "That looks like April's," he said.

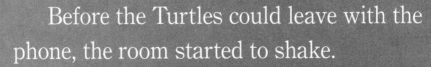

Before the Turtles could leave with the phone, the room started to shake.

Dozens of tiny robots burst through a crack in the floor. Each one grabbed a piece of loot and headed back down.

"They're stealing the stuff we stole!" Sid cried.

Fong grabbed April's phone and jumped out the window.

"B team, get him!" Leo commanded.

Mikey and Donnie were offended, but they followed Fong out the window.

Raph taunted them as they left. "Don't be afraid to call for help!"

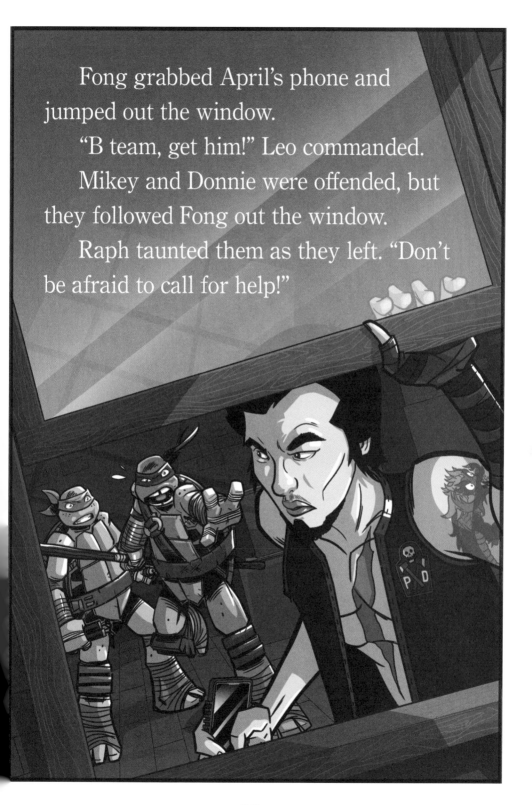

Raph and Leo smashed tiny robot after tiny robot, but many more escaped through a hole in the floor.

"Let's see where these things are coming from," Leo said, and the two Turtles jumped into the hole. Sid and Tsoi followed them.

Raph and Leo trailed the tiny robots to another building. Raph nodded at Leo, and they dropped through a skylight, landing in front of the robots' master.

"Dexter Spackman!" Raphael said.

"It's Baxter Stockman!" Baxter Stockman corrected him. "And you can't stop me.

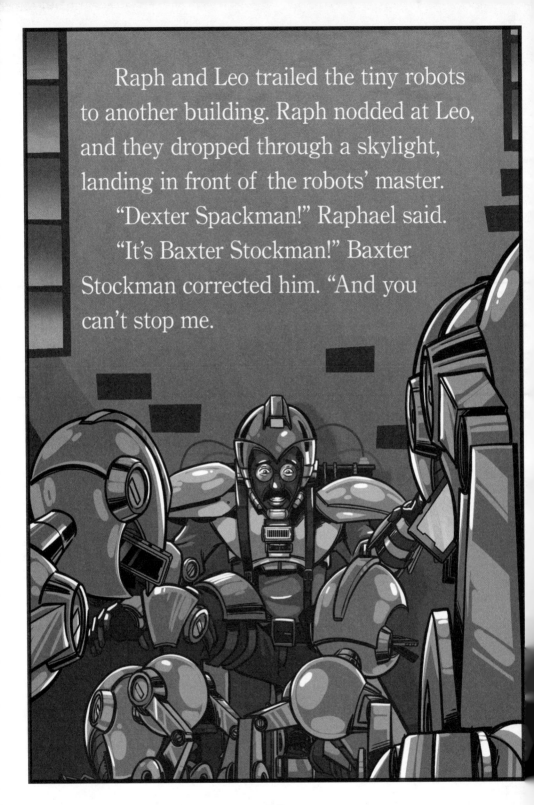

"These robots are going to make me very rich. I call them *Mousers*," he added.

Just when Raphael and Leonardo were about to attack, Baxter sprayed them with a red mist.

"Protect your eyes!" Leo cried. The two Turtles coughed and sputtered but quickly realized they were fine.

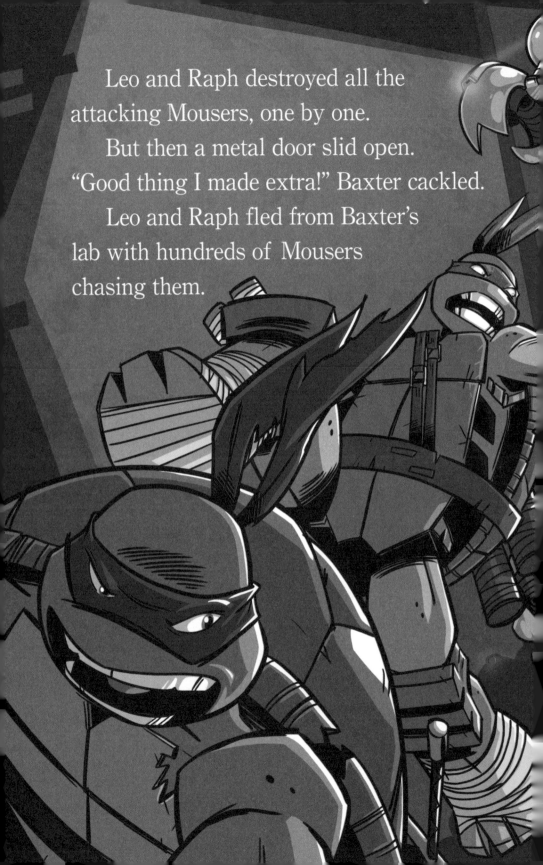

Leo and Raph destroyed all the
attacking Mousers, one by one.
    But then a metal door slid open.
"Good thing I made extra!" Baxter cackled.
    Leo and Raph fled from Baxter's
lab with hundreds of Mousers
chasing them.

Baxter was about to celebrate his victory when Sid and Tsoi jumped out of the shadows and snatched him!

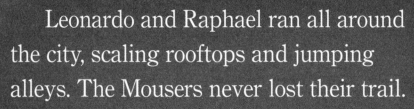

Leonardo and Raphael ran all around the city, scaling rooftops and jumping alleys. The Mousers never lost their trail.

"It must be that stuff he sprayed on us," Raph said, leaping over a fence.

"Donnie would know what to do," Leo said. But after all the teasing he and Raph had done, they were too proud to call their brother for help.

The Mousers kept coming, and Leo
and Raph kept fighting back.
"I've got an idea," Raph said.

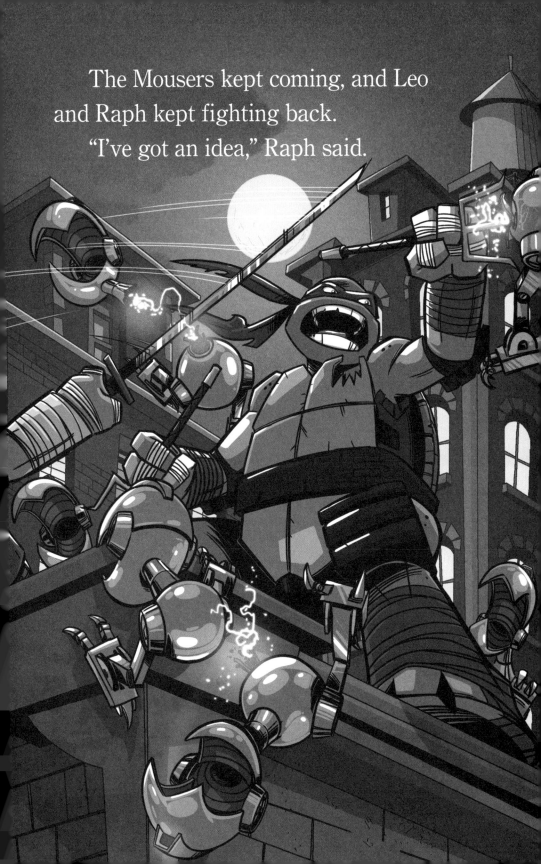

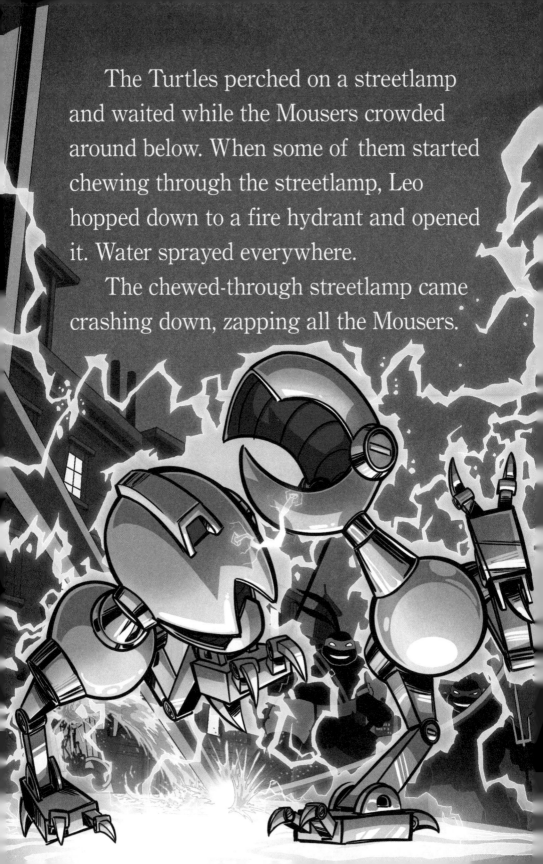

The Turtles perched on a streetlamp and waited while the Mousers crowded around below. When some of them started chewing through the streetlamp, Leo hopped down to a fire hydrant and opened it. Water sprayed everywhere.

The chewed-through streetlamp came crashing down, zapping all the Mousers.

But just when Leo and Raph thought they were safe, a new bunch of Mousers turned the corner and came after them.

"Okay, let's call Donnie," Raph said.

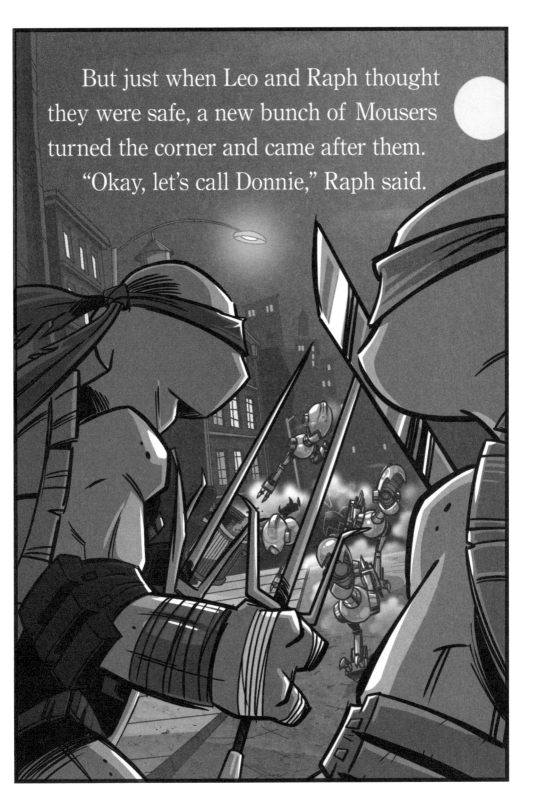

Meanwhile, Donatello and Michelangelo were following Fong to a new hideout. They watched Fong bring April's phone to Dogpound—one of the Turtles' worst enemies!

"The Turtles want this phone," Fong told him.

Dogpound tapped the screen a few times. "It's locked."

Suddenly, Sid and Tsoi entered, dragging Baxter into the hideout. Baxter's hands were tied with rope.

"This guy used robots to steal from us," Sid said.

"I don't have time for this," Dogpound said. "I have to find the Turtles."

"Turtles!" Baxter cried. "I hate those guys. My Mousers are already destroying two of them."

Dogpound raised his giant paw and brought it down hard, slashing the ropes on Baxter's hands with his claw.

Dogpound handed Baxter the phone. "If you make robots, you must be good with electronics," he said. "Hack into this."

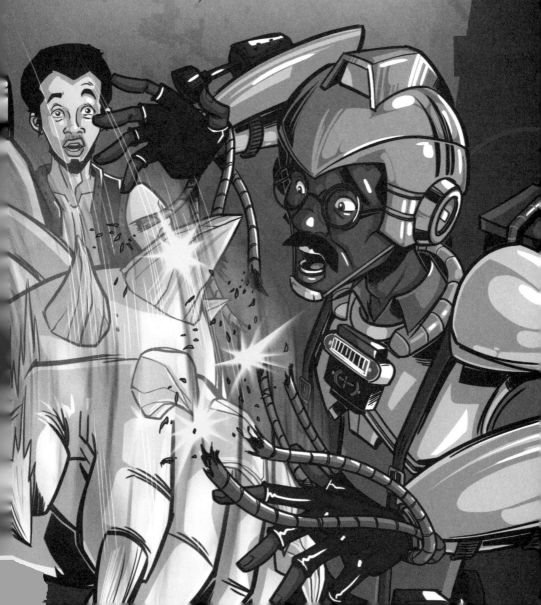

On the roof, Donatello and
Michelangelo began hatching their plan.

"We can't fight Dogpound on our own,"
Mikey said.

"You're right," Donnie said. "We'll cut
the power and snatch the phone instead."

"Operation Blackout!" Mikey
exclaimed. He loved to name things.

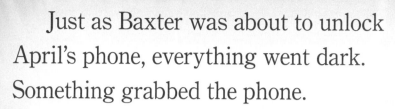

Just as Baxter was about to unlock April's phone, everything went dark. Something grabbed the phone.

Sid, Tsoi, and Baxter were confused, but Dogpound pounced. When the power came back on, he had Mikey and Donnie pinned to the floor.

Dogpound chained Donnie and Mikey to the wall. Meanwhile, Baxter kept trying to unlock April's phone.

"You're wasting your time," Donnie said.

"It has GPS on it," Baxter said. "We can see everywhere it's been."

The Turtles gasped. If Dogpound could see where their lair was, he could get Splinter!

Donnie's T-Phone started to ring. Leo and Raph were finally calling for help, but it was too late.

Dogpound grabbed Donnie's phone, and Mikey's, too. "We'll check these next," he said.

"T-Phones, self-destruct!" Donnie cried.

Pop! Hiss! The little phones sputtered and sparked in Dogpound's giant paws.

Suddenly, Raph and Leo burst through a window.

"Not so fast!" Leo called.

"How did you escape my Mousers?" Baxter asked.

"We didn't," Raph said as Mousers started pouring through a hole in the wall.

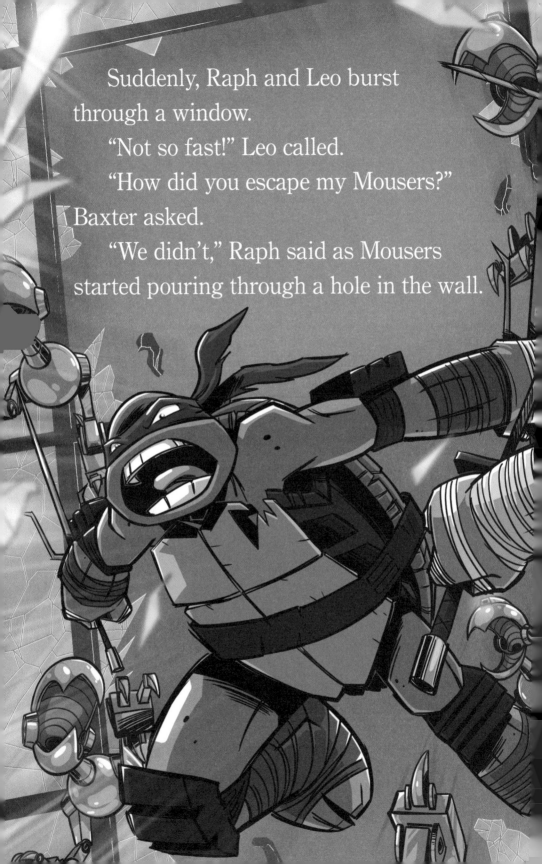

While Dogpound was distracted by
the Mousers, the Purple Dragons ran away.
Leo grabbed April's phone. Raph freed
Mikey and Donnie.

"We're here to save the day again,"
Raph teased.

"Looks like you were doing great,"
Donnie said, nodding at the Mousers.

The Turtles passed April's phone back and forth to keep it from Dogpound while trying to fend off the attacking Mousers.

"Baxter sprayed us with something," Leo told Donnie. "Now these things won't leave us alone."

Donnie picked up a smashed Mouser and looked at its insides. "A gamma camera!" he cried. "They must have sprayed you with radioisotopes. You can't get them off, but they will weaken with time. If someone else gets sprayed, though, the new signal will be stronger and attract all the Mousers."

Dogpound finally fought his way through the Mousers and charged at the Turtles. Mikey and Donnie took him on while Leo and Raph smashed the attacking Mousers.

"We need Baxter's spray," Donnie said as he blocked a strike from Dogpound.

"You mean *that*?" Mikey asked, pointing at Baxter.

Baxter stood next to Dogpound, aiming a huge red spray bottle at Mikey and Donnie.

Michelangelo flung a ninja star at Baxter's bottle. Red spray exploded all over Baxter and Dogpound.

The Mousers paused. They turned their little robot heads toward Dogpound and Baxter, sensing the new signal.

Dogpound and Baxter screamed and took off.

Dogpound snatched April's phone on his way out.

Donatello acted fast. He activated his blade and threw his staff, stabbing April's phone against the floor. It smashed to pieces.

Baxter and Dogpound ran into the night, an army of attacking Mousers right behind them.

Back at the lair, the Turtles celebrated their victory.

"Nice job, guys," Leo said.

"From now on, you're the A-minus team," Raph said.

"Well, I guess that's as good as it's going to get," said Donnie.

But Splinter was not pleased. "You chose your battle poorly and made your own problems," he said.

"We learned our lesson," Leo said. "And we did get April's phone back."

"You did?" April asked.

Leo handed April her phone—what was left of it.

"You can have one of my custom T-Phones," Donnie offered.

"Neat!" April clutched the new phone.

"Just don't say, 'T-Phone, self-destruct,'" Mikey warned.

Pop! Hiss!